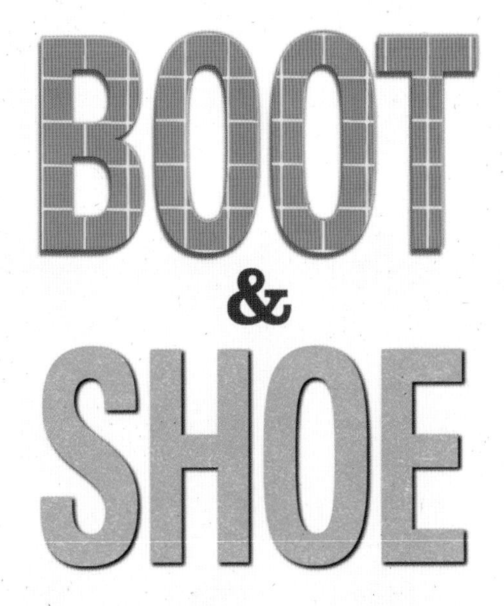

Marla Frazee

SIMON AND SCHUSTER
London New York Sydney Toronto New Delhi

To Steve Malk, who likes cats more

SIMON AND SCHUSTER
First published in Great Britain in 2012
by Simon and Schuster UK Ltd
1st Floor, 222 Gray's Inn Road,
London, WC1X 8HB
A CBS Company

Originally published in 2012
by Beach Lane Books,
an imprint of Simon and Schuster
Children's Publishing Division, New York

A CIP catalogue record for this book is
available from the British Library upon request

ISBN: 978-0-85707-925-1 (HB)
ISBN: 978-0-85707-926-8 (PB)

Printed in China

10 9 8 7 6 5 4 3 2 1
www.simonandschuster.co.uk

Boot and Shoe were born into the same litter,
and now they live in the same house.

They eat
dinner out of
the same bowl.

They pee on
the same tree.

At night, they sleep in the same bed.

But Boot spends his days on the back porch,
because he's a back porch kind of dog.

And Shoe spends his days on the front porch,
because he's a front porch kind of dog.

This is exactly
perfect for
both of them.

Then one day,

for no apparent reason,

a squirrel started
some
trouble.

It chattered
at Boot.

It chattered
at Shoe.

It threw stuff
at Boot.

It threw stuff
at Shoe.

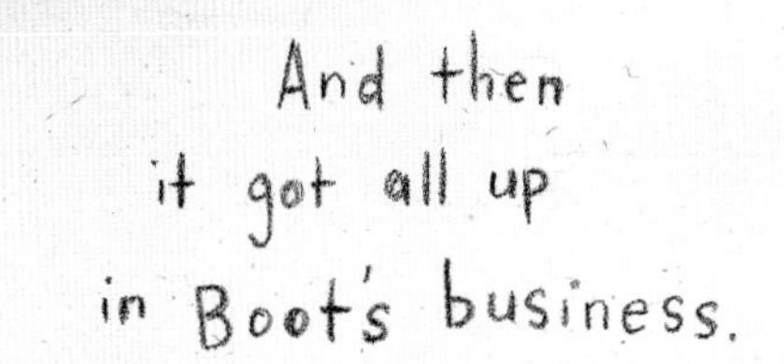

And then
it got all up
in Boot's business.

And it got
all up in
Shoe's business,
too.

Whoa.

Something had
to be done.

So Boot and Shoe
chased that squirrel
all over the place.

They chased it and
chased it and
chased it
until it
got
bored
and
walked
away.

Boot collapsed.

Shoe collapsed, too.

When Boot
opened his eyes,
he saw that he was on the front porch.
He looked around for Shoe.
Shoe should be here.
But he wasn't.

Oh, no.

When
Shoe
opened his
eyes, he saw that he was on the back porch.
He looked around for Boot.
Boot should be here.
But he wasn't.

Oh, no.

Boot searched
the front porch for Shoe.
He looked under things,
over things,
around things,
and between
things.

No luck.

Shoe searched
the back porch for Boot.
He looked under things,
over things,
around things,
and between
things.

No luck
for him
either.

Boot decided to station himself on the front porch and wait there until Shoe found his way back.

And Shoe decided to station himself on the back porch and wait there until Boot found his way back.

It was
a long,
lonely
afternoon.

When it was dinnertime, Boot's stomach rumbled.
But he didn't want to eat dinner without Shoe.

Shoe's stomach rumbled, too.
But he didn't want to eat dinner without Boot.
It was a long,
hungry evening.

At bedtime, Boot was shivering.
But he didn't want to get in bed without Shoe.

Shoe was shivering, too.
But he didn't want to get in bed
without
Boot.

Once during the night,
Boot walked slowly around
to the back porch
to see if Shoe
was
there,

and Shoe
walked slowly
around to the front porch
to see if Boot was there.

But no luck again.

So Boot ended up back on the front porch waiting for Shoe,

and Shoe ended up back on the back porch waiting for Boot.

It was
a long,
sleepless
night.

The sun came up.

On the
front porch,
there was still no sign of Shoe.
Boot began to cry.

On the
back porch,
there was still no sign of Boot.
Shoe began to cry, too.

But, even in
the worst of times,
a dog still needs
to pee.

Boot dragged
himself over
to the tree.

Shoe dragged
himself over
to the tree,
too.

And suddenly, lo and behold, there they were again!

Overjoyed to see each other!

Overtired, too.

So even though the day was just beginning, Boot and Shoe decided

that the exact perfect thing for both of them to do was go right to bed.

Together!

(Of course.)